BETWEEN
THE
GATES

BETWEEN THE GATES

DAVID ADAMSON

PROLOGUE

Hellish Standing on the Bridge

Guided permission is actually used with permission. For, from the source everything cometh, that Fountain Head, where The Universe springs fourth into the vastness of nothing. What was once priceless is becoming worthless. What was once worthless is becoming priceless. The Goddesses, set in place a veil, between the living and the dead. That veil is all that protects me now as I cross over that connection between life, and the solace of the soul. While aboard the bridge, while still in control of my being, protected from the elements that lie ahead, just out of reach. I perceive the progression; Angels, Demons, Grim Reapers, as The Pale Horse rides out across the landscape of an ancient battlefield. I am standing on that bridge beside a powerful Hells' Angel, wisps of smoke and steam drift from him. His coal black eyes leak a bluish vapor caused by the burning damned souls still in him. He doesn't know that I am there, because of the fog that encloses me. I scream out, but no one hears me. Death surrounds me, as I bear witness to the suffering of the multitude below. Just then I am aware that you see me standing there. The realization is immediate, that bridge exists in all of our minds. I am on it, and you see me.

22/07/16

HELL'S GATE. Sometimes it looks like this. Sometimes it looks like that. Sometimes it's different all together. When you're a soul being brought here, you will know when you get there, exactly where you are. You will know, through that Gate lies your end. I know that you've heard all those fucked up stories about Hell. Well, when you get here, yes you might get burnt. Yes, you might get chopped up. Yes, you might get torn apart. And yes, you might be led through the Gate by a Hell's Angel. You might get taken into Hell and then given a guided tour. What the fuck were you expecting to happen? HELL wants the essence from your soul, then you will be lost. Occasionally, a Hell's Angel may find a soul to be one of us, and will start the process of changing you into a Hell's Angel. I tell everyone, "Don't be pissing off people on Earth. Because when you get to Hell, you might need a friend. Your friends on Earth will tell you "that they will back you all the way to Hell's Gate", and they mean it. Then the chicken shit bastards will turn and run for Heaven, (as if they will get in there). I however will back you through the Gates of Hell. I will back you while you are in Hell. What the fuck, I'll even get you a guided fuck'n tour of the place. I'm a Hells' Angel, I get being dead. I'm so dead, the dead in Hell are fucking scared of me. The Demons and Furies are fucking scared of me. You are fucking scared of me. In Hell we are all dead, lost, and we 'get', being dead. And now that you are here too. It's time you get being dead. These are the lines you will find written on signposts along the road to Hell. The Angels of Hell wrote these signposts, with still smoldering clawed hands when they were first created in Hell. The essence stolen from them was used to create these great creatures from the fires in Hell along with the poisons, toxins and hallucinogenic material, being stored up from the silk road through the portal in Babylon. Present day peoples such as you read and are familiar with the name Babylon, but it has a much more ancient past. The old city was called Akkadian. It was controlled by Africa, The Amazons, and in the day, Addas Abba was the central power of the Goddesses peoples.

25/03/17

When the Goddesses were in the Heavens, and people followed Mother Earth. Hell had no power. Hell was part of the cosmos. Hell has always been in the Heavens. Hell has been waiting for a future event that would provide a source of power. The Goddesses built the Heavens, all life in all galaxies were led by them. Goddesses know that their very existence is,' life quintessential'. Goddesses were replaced by Gods on Earth. At a point when Mankind split up into large governing groups, controlled by burgeoning bureaucracies. Gods began to appear everywhere. People used the knowledge gained from the Goddesses against each other as part of deal making. For the first time in Man's 'history', the *tool* was not in the hand but in the other man's mind. When that tool malfunctioned, people suffered and died. Thus, deals were broken, distrust, jealousy and hatred became common conditions in the mind of mankind. Goddesses remained strong only where humanity first came into contact with Mother Earth. Mankind's groups spread out across what is now Asia, Europe, and the Americas. As kingdoms sprung up, with the help of bureaucracies, Gods moved across the land, and many became convinced that the true power was in the 'Fight', for power. Wars broke out, the lesser were trod upon, and great nation building began. Gods rebelled against Man, at points when mankind distrusted his God. All the while, Hell was gathering souls in great numbers. HELL, felt that when the Goddesses were pushed out, great power would be inevitable. Great wars also sprung up in the Heavens. Then came the quest for immortality, and the Silk Road. Mankind's use of hallucinogenic drugs to manipulate the brain's frequency. The Goddesses were driven off, the Gods fought *Gallantly*, mankind created monsters. Immortality was within the grasp of man… God struck a deal with HELL… The Fixer was locked up in Hell. The "

Great Test " began, an eternity passed. I escaped, I returned with the Mako to this place. All the Gods were here warring, the Earth was BOILING. The Mako exposed the Truth there.

The Mako, after standing between the Gates of Heaven and Hell, struck the peach seed, for the coming of the 'Peach Festival'. The truth of immortality, and the usage of souls was exposed. This set off man's next quest. To find the soul, to find Heaven and to find HELL. In other words, the 'source' of ultimate power and to gain control over it, or risk total annihilation of everything in the process. The Mako moved to be with the *Peoples'* of Earth, as they transformed themselves, just as she transformed herself when the Ghost of Hell was expelled from her. I began my quest to find the Mako with a ' Bitch of Hell, one of Babylon's Angels. She led me to the crossroads in Heaven. God struck her dead; I was given the location of the Mako. I was **banished** from Heaven.

Now, I step into Hell with the carcass of a dead Hell's Angel. A pull on the atmosphere in Hell, then a bubble appears and opens, I step out into HELL. On my back are the Heaven's wings that were given to me, and the reason I emerge from a bubble. I am grasping the carcass of a dead Hell's Angel; I hang in the atmosphere of Hell. Just then, Hells' Angels flash from Heaven where I was just before. My protector, her protector, plus the other two that followed along with their protector Angels. In an instant the carcass turns to *dust* and disperses. Hell's orange tinted atmosphere hangs overhead. Beneath lies the ever-flowing' **STYX'**. There is the line of souls, marching towards the River Styx, and on the farthest banks, the lost souls moan and drift out and away from the '**River of The Damned'**. There are layers of colour bands in the atmosphere, caused by hallucinogens, toxins and poisonous gases.

More Hells' Angels appear, Furies, Hellhounds, and Demons move in great numbers below me. HELL speaks," Fixer ! You are **Not** one of us now ! You dawn of the wings of Heaven. Your purpose here is **Finished!**" " You will, however, bring the Mako to the banks of the STYX, now that she can be found." I can't imagine your replacement, only **one** of you can exist in the universe at the same time. Bring the Mako here! Be prepared to' *Fight"* for your place in the universe, and your position at the battle of 'Evermore." "HELL has no use for an Angel with wings from Heaven!..." I fly through Hell, I howl, I pass over the River STYX, just skimming the surface. Souls in line gesture in my direction. It's the wings I have, they do not cower in fear like before. The other Angels that fly with me, **scream** and **howl** at the souls. I imagine the Mako, surfing the STYX with her *shield*. The smoke, the ash, piled up on the riverbanks. The souls seeing the *truth* beneath the STYX, and disappearing. I am a Hells' Angel, I am made of **Hate**, I feel **nothing**. Heaven's wings or not. I am a duality; I can be as a God. I move amongst these other Angels with a grace not available to them. I strike out at them, they fight back. The ones that try to protect Hell get in on the Fray. I fucking kill some of them. Fuck Hell, Fuck Hells' Angels, Fuck the souls here in Hell. We Fight each other, we *FIGHT* **For HELL...!** I fly straight up now, bored with this struggle. I must seek the Mako. I fly upwards through the orange tinted sky of Hell. I flash my wings. I step into a bubble, I exit Hell. **IT** can't hold me, nor can **IT** follow me. I will be followed by my protector. This will be fuckin awesome!

13/06/17

I portal out over the Aegean Sea. I came here to experience the results of the testing from the Silk Road. To the North and West of the Aegean, lies the Greatest of the New Kingdoms on Earth. The Olympians have 'Cities of Lights', above the Earth. They have come here to spread their vision of conquest among Man. Civilization building is taking hold in this land. **Demi** Gods live on the Earth. Vampires, Werewolves, Shapeshifters, and tall monsters live throughout the region. I drift above the crystal-clear waters. My protector Angel moves with me. The coastal areas are strikingly beautiful. I can sense the presence of the Gods of Olympia. They dare not confront me. I will fuck'n rip them into shreds if they do try…! Their Underworld God, Hades, lived in Hell during these days. HELL made good use of Hades' Appearance. I came to this area to avoid detection by, or of Babylon. I am moving Eastward along the Northern Coast. I am in no hurry. My protector is nervous, anxious, bothered by the Olympians. It wants to fight; the Fucking Thing better Hold Position!. Distractions and attention are not what is at hand here. I seek only the Mako. I must move among Mankind, not their Gods. Their Gods fear my presence, but don't fear me. They should, but their *arrogance* is what got them here. I howl at my protector, striking at him. Making him aware of his lack of attention to our mission. Stay on course!

I am a Hells' Angel; I emit steam and smoke trails, from my burnt flesh. I wear wings from Heaven now, I still leak a bluish mist from my coal black eyes. I am made of Hate. My protector is beginning to draw attention to our position. I summon more Hells' Angels. Two flash to our position with two protectors. Then a pull on the atmosphere, as the atmosphere splits, a portal opens, and a Heavens' Angel steps out. More portals appear. All together eight of Heaven's Angels take up positions alongside us. When I summoned the Hells' Angels, the wings I wear, summoned Heaven's accompaniment. I quickly bring the five from Hell into line with me. I cannot afford any confrontation with the Olympians or our support. We move over what will become Troy. Then out over the Black Sea. The Angels of Babylon were always there, even in those days. Babylon has a much more ancient past. At this time, the portal to Hell is established. Souls are gathered from all along the Silk Road, where it leads into many different and distant cultures. At this time, Babylon's name is Akkadian. Monsters, Werewolves, and Vampires run amuck. Man has started to look for the 'self. The conscience: not the soul, or his god, and man has worshipped many Gods. It's an amazing site. The Olympians, the Cities of Lights, that hang in the sky. The Gods here are beautiful. I watch as Poseidon moves, part sea, part sky, awesome and graceful. Our group is striking as we pass by. Hells' Angels, made of Hate. Smoke and steam drift from us. Coal black eyes, so focused that you can only see dead lost souls burning behind the blackness.

The Heaven's Angels glisten from their armour, the golden hair, the brilliance given off their swords made of lightning. The shields have a heavenly glow. I can see Poseidon's reflection in the sea water shields. The beautiful gleaming Heaven's Angels have the most beautiful wings, God's power is in their wings. They wear a thin sheep slipper on their feet. A silk glove on their hands, made from the silkworm. The finest found in China, and made available to the Silk Road. The sounds of bells ring, slivers of light move through the skies. When God's Angels move above the Earth, the skies rejoice. The birds sing, fog appears and diminishes. Animals on the land stop for an instant, looking heavenward to the Angels in flight. We move on over the Black Sea. Then pass over the Caucasus Mountains, to the Caspian Sea, then beyond into and over Pakistan, finally into India to the Hindu Kush. The Himalayan Mountains also known as the Mythological Kunlun. Angels have no sense of time. Traveling across the Earth does not take time as it is known to man. The speed they travel is not measurable. Angels are focused on souls, and years move forward and backward in their vision, ' like colors in the lenses of the senses' as they make passage. Our trip here is one of mystery, and truth. The Mako has found a truth here, and the' Peach Festival' is begun by these peoples. The mystery is how man forges his history from the Earth. The elixir of immortality is flowing down the Silk Road. Gods, Spirits, demons, and shapeshifters play with the immortals. The hallucinogenic plants in the area of the Kunlun make it possible for the shamans to watch and make contact with the spirit world. Man is looking for the elixir of the soul. Man knows that when the body dies, the brain holds no memories or thoughts. There is no proof that the conscience or self was ever in the physical mind of the dead body. Man is already reaching for God's power at this early time! The fires of Hell are licking at my feet, they constantly **burn** the body of a Hell's Angel. It's one of the reasons that I emit smoke and steam as I pass over the Earth. The entire group of us are high above the Himalayas as we approach from the North. Gods from the East have been watching our approach. Mythological beasts move along our path. Dragons fly along the valley edges. Large serpents move in the waters. Man has built along the rock buttresses that jut up from the river edges. Crop lands are scattered along the valley's floor. Smoke drifts in the air from the fires burning in villages. We are drifting in time as we move through this area. The Mako passed through these lands. I move to the passage of soul building and the time man first pursued the 'Peach Festival. The *Sands* of *Time* were spilled in Heaven, not Hell. I can move to a time of my choosing, the years and seasons on Earth pass quickly. And like colours in the' lenses of the senses', come and go without emotion to a Hells' Angel. Man cannot see us, nor the Gods that gather. The beasts do not hinder us, our focus is not lost, we fly on.

I am a Heaven's Angel. Made of milk and honey, long golden hair, eyes of blue diamond. My wings have the power of God, they are indestructible. I have a sword of lightning in one hand and a shield, made of sea water held within a portal, in the other. Slippers of sheepskin and gloves of the finest silk. I have portaled out at the beginning of the 'Battle of Evermore'. I have been sent here to bring an end to HELL. I am high above the Earth, the sky all around is filled with Angels. Lightning flashes, tiny lights glisten, eyes, all of them. Black as coal, the eyes of Hell's Angels that are mixed with all of us. Their eyes emit a bluish vapor, and a spark of light from the great flash. God! Why have you sent me here?! I can not move! I cannot feel my sword, I can not move my wings! In front of me, is a Hell's Angel. Souls burn in his head. Hate is all that fills his being. I want to fly at the thing!, I want to sever his limbs, and release the souls trapped in him. I can feel his hate, I am losing my grip on everything around me now. I hang in the air effortlessly; but my wings are still. My mane flows down without feeling. The beads of Holy water that are sprinkled on my body, shimmer off the light from the great spark. I don't know if I can hold this position much longer. The Hell's Angel in front of me, doesn't seem to be able to move either. The monster looks, feels and smells like Hell. I feel it's hate, I see the puffs of smoke, and steam that drifts from it. I smell the acrid odor as the whiffs of smoke drift past. I can sense the empty black hole, where the heart should be.

I watch as sparks drift past, where are they coming from? The battle of Evermore is here and now, beneath us, Earth is alive with change. The Goddesses have come, gone, the Gods have come,and gone. The monsters have played with the immortals. Man has rooted his power in an infertile soil. Now the water is tainted, the ground is barren, and the air is insipid. I am still hanging in the air amongst Angels in numbers not fathomable. Amongst Gods of old, Goddesses of the past. Monsters are assembled, immortals gathered, giant beats and dragons. Still the sparks drift past. Tiny embers glowing flicker, and at times becoming translucent. I look directly at the Hell's Angel before me. I can see the reflection of a spark in the coal black dead eyes. The bluish vapor that leaks out reminds me of the souls that are burning in his head. I feel that just as the spark passes, so will this, this inability to carry out this battle. Then I see the gathering, the gathering of the sparks. They are all drifting to one place. It is the beginning of something. The ebb and flow has just exposed us at the end.

I am the Fixer; I have been from the beginning of time to the end of time. I am here at the front line of the' Battle of Evermore'. HELL, has gathered as many souls as it can to the end of time for this battle. I have frozen everything! I am looking at an Angel from Heaven. Long golden blonde hair, blue diamond eyes, lightning sword and a portal of sea water shield. God's armour laid on her body, so brilliant that it would kill anything!, except me.

A Hell's Angel is protected form the armour." Mako! Where are you?" I watch a spark drift past. Sparkles of light dance on the beads of holy water on the Heaven's Angel before me. Monsters, Demons, immortals, Gods and Goddesses of past! I want to kill them all! I want to rip all that is left to shreds! I am made of hate! I'm dead, I'm so fucking dead that the dead in HELL fear me. Dead lost souls burn in my head. The fires of Hell lick constantly at my feet. I still remember walking the road to Hell. The road burns with words glowing in every language known to man. The words are as bricks each glowing with Hell fire. The sides of the road are marked with signposts. Some have been made of bone fused with stone. The souls are led down this road to Hell by the Angels of Hell. Hell's mercenaries; the Grim Reapers, Angel's of Death. The soul of man, so mystical. The breath of the universe, a source of essence beyond all the Gods and Goddesses. The soul carries with it the conscience of being, it pours from the FountainHead of the Universe. From this very spout, the Gods and Goddesses were created. This is why the road to Hell is burning words. The Word, the Logos, the Christ. The way to Hell is burning the soul into the waste flowing in the STYX. The signposts along the road to HELL were written by the Angels of Hell when first they were created and still smoldering. The souls read these signs and 'directed', they will soon be lost.

As I walked the road to HELL, I recited the words on the signposts, recognizing the breath of me was the spirit of the fountain head of the universe. I gathered strength from the other's passing between the gates into Hell, I transformed into a Hells' Angel. Then I immediately began to Rage throughout Hell; gathering vapor for my fiery flight. What the fuck, a spark drifts past my eyes! A fucking spark, in Hell? This place is on fire, smoldering ashes blow everywhere. The atmosphere is pungent, gasses billow and propagate amongst the hallucinogenic laden gaseous atmosphere. The spark then stopped, diffused into millions of sparks. The Diaphanous One appears before Hell. Creates the illusion of infinity from a spark. When the brilliance went away, I found myself in chains, anchored to the floor of a cell, with only one barred window to let in light, and a heavy door. This is how I found myself locked up for eternity. A spark drifts past. Another spark drifts past. I'm in Hell, I know where I am. I remember how I got here. I remember tracing the words on the signposts along the road to Hell. When I was created, still smoldering from Hell fire. I can still feel the poisonous STYX filling my soul and hallucinogenic vapor reorganizing the mental aggregate of Hell itself, creating the Fixer. Hell envisioned the Fixer; the spark, was the diaphanous one, come to Hell to lay down the great test, and seal my fate at the front line of the Battle of Evermore.

03/06/17

My long blonde golden mane hangs, still. My blue diamond eyes shine with the truth and empathy, my skin is milky and covered with God's armour. Beads of holy water glisten here and they're on me. My silk gloves are brilliant, they have the lustrous glow now as do my sheepskin slippers. The sheen is that of vivid purity. I am Heaven's Angel; I carry a sword of lightning and a shield made of sea water held in a portal constructed by God. The taste of me is of the best honey, to touch me is to make the feel of milk on my skin. Now, I have the truth child with me. I am The Mako. Not of this Earth, not the duality that once possessed the ghost of HELL. I am not even fused with the Heavens. I am separated from all that is, because of the truth child and this duality that now exists. I am moving with the people of the Earth. These people are in and of transposition. I am also in and of transposition. After having taken part in the beginning of the Peach Festival, with the peoples of the land of the Gods. The Gods and Goddesses all gathered to witness the unfolding of Mankind's transition towards understanding immortality, with the use of an elixir. During that time in man's history the Aryan people were in great numbers, with vast resources. They moved out of India into China and worked their way Eastward, towards the ocean. The numbers of them are truly magnificent. The movement was like that of a party, 100's of 1000's. All together these groups exceed 10's of millions of people moving en masse. Signing, chanting. dancing: flags fly high above the people. They pull kites even higher into the sky above them. Fires are built and some fires spread out onto the surrounding countryside.

06/07/17

I am The Mako traveling with these people. Their journey is a combination, one of mystery and purpose. Never before in Man's history or for that matter, never again will so many people migrate across continents with such jubilation and sedulousness. Never before has there been The Mako amongst the people on Earth, while Goddesses travel with the creation of souls in pursuit of wisdom and truth. Rainbows appear as storms abate; the Goddesses travel on these rainbows. Angels of God travel among the people, both above and below the Earth's surface. The sheer number of animals that move with these people is breathtaking! I fly above the people as they move. The sky is full of kites, banners, flags, smoke, birds Angels, insects. Fires burn, torches are lit, as night descends on the travelers the land turns to a hallucinatory, disorienting dream state. The surreal state of being is, and has a universal continuance. In that the cosmos is in flux, and at times movements of whole galaxies band together and strike out into the heavenly bodies. As Man's jubilance spreads out across the land, so does the heavenly movement of Goddesses and Gods. The land to the East of the Himalayas is populated with large numbers of people. The challenges are many. These people struck out, fully prepared for acceptance, or conflict. Movements of people this large cause many changes to the shape of both the land, and the peoples' that reside upon it. Roads are built, bridges are constructed. New and large dwellings are erected. All are subsequently used, reused, and much logistical knowledge is learnt by both the traveler and the indigenous inhabitants.

Watching these events unfold I am taken with Mankind's ability to regenerate, and together with the speed of adaptiveness to geography and environmental challenges. It's like watching a leaf fall from a tree onto a perfectly still pond. The ripples move out from the landing of the leaf, magically timed and self replicating. Changes happen like this in the heavenly bodies in the cosmos. Information is passed from one physical state to another, like memories stored in the mind. Man is moving towards the understanding of Immortality. Transcendence is moving, moving and understanding movement is transcendence. The fluidity of the mass is a reflection of the cosmos in real life. And this 'life' that is mimicking the cosmos, is the breeding ground for the souls. I watch the stunning beauty of large numbers of people, animals, changes to landscape; all the while rain, wind, sunshine, nighttime, shooting stars and meteors fly by. Cities of lights appear, wars breakout on the land, I am watching wars breakout amongst the Goddesses and Gods that are gathering. These Gods are challenging the Goddesses and their position in the Heavens. This transition is why I am here, I have the Truth Child within me. I am a duality of Truth and Child. A combination, a binary system, a 'Pure Radical'. This place, this moment in Man's journey will be the testing ground for the Mako. The Earth is being tested by the entourage flowing out of the warring Gods and Goddesses. Tested by the environment in the solar system, tested by entourage flowing out of the warring Gods and Goddesses. Tested by geological change from within. The Truth Child is tested to learn the truth of Man's ability to understand immortality.

07/11/17

I fly over the land, people, and the beauty of the landscape. I can feel Heaven and the souls that pass by. Angels perform a multitude of tasks during their appointments. Among these, are the movement of souls to heaven, after the time of death by someone who lived on the land. I am used to seeing an Angel providing a soul with a stairway to Heaven. For a moment it looks like Kayos all around, I am jarred back to the moment; as I pass over a battlefield. I see groups of Angels departing with souls towards Heaven. The souls themselves are beautiful, in that they look like small rainbows with specks of dust flickering inside. Angels from Heaven convince the souls to travel with them by placing the rainbow into their long blonde hair like a ribbon or bow. Together they strike out for Heaven. The spectacle unfolds over and over en masse beneath me. I drift serene, as I pass over the battlefield. Angels notice me, the souls also notice me. I appear as a source of brilliance and tranquility. Never seen before by Angels or the souls. I am The Mako. I am sagaciously intertwined with the Truth Child. The Heavens Angels have never witnessed the Mako take flight. I am concerned with the Kayos of the battlefield. The unimaginable horror goes on unabated in waves of human subversion. Hellhounds roam the battlefield, they run with the 'Dogs of War'. Their aim. to distract, confuse, or delay any of the soldiers who may notice. These men and women of war are focused on what, or who lies ahead, they consume many types of hallucinogens. These plants and herbs are found readily available.

08/30/17

Preparations for battle include, the knowledge of the effects of stimulants on the body; and moreover, the mind. During battle the benefits include: high pain tolerance, increase in strength, mobility, and although not intentionally, in combination this can cause some to catch a glimpse of immortality. The physical self bridges the gap to the soul via a virtual connection created by the combination of hallucinogen, and mental acuity due to deprived spiritual awareness. These change the frequency of the mind; this is the bridge. I am on that bridge. I am standing there for you to see me. I am The Mako, the Truth Child is with me on that bridge. Together we are a combination, brilliance and child. Truth and Serenity. Never before have I stood on that bridge in the mind. never before have the Gods nor the Goddesses witnessed me across that bridge. I witness the soul's passage from the 'living' to Heaven. Then I stand on that bridge and witness the Grim Reapers appear. The Pale Horse, the Hells' Angels. This is the start of the removal of God's power from the soul to Hell. The Hells' Angel cuts the soul from its connection to life, like a strike from a blade of a razor. The soul is stripped from its life source and impaled on the Hells' Angel; many souls can be gathered in this fashion. A Hells' Angel may gather hundreds, or thousands of souls impaled on his encrusted burnt flame. The Reaper of Souls, the Pale Horse. The war of man goes on beneath me as I fly over. I am concerned with the passage of souls. I am standing on a bridge for souls between Gates.

I run, meaning: I am a horse! My mane trails, long and golden behind me. In it I have gathered rainbows with specks of dust. Souls, so attracted to me, because of my serenity. I am not the bearer of passage. But the souls watch me on the bridge, and I can not refuse them. I am The Mako. I am an Angel meant for the immortality of people and I run. Souls gather in my hair, and I pass over the battlefield on a bridge Between Gates. The Gates of Heaven and Hell. I recite the Creed: I WILL, Promise, to PROTECT, and TRUST every soul created. Will, Promise, Protection and Trust. The four truths that must be sworn by 'every Angel created. I run, my armour glistens in the glow from fires on the land, and the bright moon light from above. The beads of holy water glisten, my shield reflects light from sparks that are drifting past. I cross the bridge and into the Gates of Heaven. The souls immediately transform into the malleable spirits that grace the golden streets; the redeemer cleanses these streets by absorbing the sin of man. The diaphanous one moves to be with the Mako, the Holy Spirit (the transparent one) is within. I am The Mako, I am serene, pure, eyes of the best blue diamond, my skin makes milk when touched, and the taste of me is the best honey from a honeycomb. My long blonde hair drapes to my knees, I wear silk gloves from the finest silkworm and thin sheepskin slippers about my feet. I hold a sword made of lightning and a portal that holds a whole sea of saltwater as a shield. I am covered by God's pure armour and beads of holy water are sprinkled here and there.

I am The Mako, a Heaven's Angel, in combination with the Truth Angel. A duality, I am a God, I am more powerful than even the Fixer Angel from Hell. I have separated from the Fixer to be with the people on Earth that move towards transposition. I have returned to Heaven. I have returned souls to this place of absolute pristine elegance and grace. The souls flicker and sparks are everywhere. Small translucent glowing particles drift past me, seemingly appearing from nowhere, all gathering in one spot. Then a blinding flash and the diaphanous one appears from inside the flash. There looks to be dust or sand on the street under the God before me. I have stood many times before in this place, on these streets of gold. Never before have I seen sand on the street. I am aware that change is upon Heaven. The Pearl Nautilus has been without age as long as I have known it. However, this time I am sure an age has moved through Heaven. The diaphanous one speaks to me; " Mako, you have come. You have come bearing souls for Heaven. You have not accompaniment the Fixer. I am informing you that the 'Sands of Time' have been split in Heaven during your absence. No! Do not step on the sand, or time will pass for you as well. You are not affected by the passage of time as of yet. The Fixer brought an Angel of Babylon here, searching you out. For you that time has not occurred, you must not touch the sand at my feet, as you still have to travel with the Aryan peoples. The Fixer was able to get your exact location from me. I was unable to protect your position as time passed here, and on Earth. The Fixer will come for you Mako! The Fixer will deliver you to HELL!".

08/03/17

This is a dream, the sands of time here in Heaven. This is a dream; TIME., has passed me by here in Heaven. This is a dream! I reach out with my sword and stroke, (time passes) the street. A blue flame is emitted and smoke appears, the diaphanous one shimmers. A Golden Rod appears before me. "Stop, Stop now! The Angel from Babylon stroked the street before, as you are doing now. Stop! The Mako, is a powerful Angel now, Even, 'so powerful, as powerful as a God. The Mako, will not be the pawn of any deal made on Earth, in Hell or Heaven. I stroke the street, because the golden path is the way of 'the one that walks on water'. 'The Logos, the Word'. The road to HELL is paved with words like bricks, laid down in a Hellish quicksand. A sand so designed to trap souls, lost souls that burn and moan from within the sand. And their words are in every language known to Mankind. These words were once spoken by their religious leaders on Earth. I know that by stroking the golden street with my sword. The one that walks on water will appear and repair the road at my feet. The Way, and the Word of Christ will be cleansed, so that," I may come closer to you, so I may be instructed by your governance, as to the meaning of my time on Earth". Mako! Stop! I tell you now. The damage done to the golden street by the Angel from Hell is permanent. Once the time has passed, I can not take it back. You cannot approach me, or the passage of time will consume you, your mission on Earth will cease, and you will find yourself in a pyre on the banks of the river STYX at once! I cannot instruct you: not now Mako".

I back away from my God. I sense his grace, but may not commune with my God. The goldenrod is with-drawn. I notice a grain of sand just in front of me, I point my sword at it. The granule sparkles, I become empowered by the position I now have. I know, I will return to the battlefield, I will find one more truth, and the Fixer will find me as time goes by on Earth, and God will instruct me. The sands of time are running out of a portal in Hell. I have seen them there, when I held a Ghost of Hell in my head, Whilst I surfed the STYX. That is the place where souls go, as part of their suffrage. To be as cement, lost in the road to HELL. As I walk away from the diaphanous one, a glowing light burns behind me, God is flashing. I then notice a glowing spark pass by in front of me, I reach for it. I hear bells ringing in the distance, I notice the beautiful black sky and rainbows in the distance. Stars fill the Heavenly ceiling above, then I ponder, as the glowing spark passes through my hand, I am not in Heaven, I am not here. I am in a dream. The spark dances on the beads of Holy water about me. A breeze kicks up dust and leaves from the road's edges, they blow through me. The spark moves ahead of me, I run for it, I reach for it. I flash my wings, a portal forms, a bubble opens. I step into and out over a battlefield, the air splits behind me with a deafening clamor. The Pale Horse is at my side. He is beautiful, he is hideous, he is focused on man's discharge of his soul. Still, I reach out for that spark as it drifts just out of my reach. The stench of the battle, the screams, I am caught up in the battle.

08/04/17

The scene unfolding below is 'Breathtaking. Warriors move in timed succession. Some carry large flags, some pull streamers. Large groups dance as they progress across the open expanse of grassland. Far ahead the frontline of battle is in Flux. The use of Giants and large animals is part of the illusion set forth. There are groups of spearmen, heavily armored. Lighter agile men with bow and arrows follow, some carry a hinged throwing device, constantly picking up stones and hurling them into the air. As the larger animals, elephants, oxen, bears, boars, tigers, lions, horses become injured. They go mad, and in death throws, can clear from a couple to as many as

20 front line soldiers. These large animals seem to be placed at intervals, respective to groups of lightweight fighters. They are used as pack animals, then they serve as position cracking devices, and shield advancing fighters. Then when they become enraged, they are set upon the enemy frontline. Fires are set and smoke also shields advancing soldiers from held recon positions. The Aryan Peoples are moving across this land in large numbers. At the forefront are legions of men, soldiers, and innumerable amounts and types of animals. There are small kites and very large kites. Banners, streamers, the whole movement has a party like atmosphere. However, at this locale, the native inhabitants are opposed to the advance of such a large troop. The local inhabitants have been aware of the progression for some time, and have procured a formidable force, with the hopes of deflecting the progression away from their lands. However, they are logistically unable to meet the needs of their frontline, and the encroaching army has the means of re-supply.

Just in front of me, seems like only a few feet. The spark that followed me throughout the portal is leading the way as I glide alongside the Hell's Angel. His mission here is collecting souls for Hell. His eyes black, shine of the dead, a bluish glow and are fixed on the mission before him, He won't confront me as his focus is fixed; if he were to, I would gladly release all the souls burning in him, and the ones impaled on him. Still, he moves like a juggernaut amongst the other demons, dragons and hell hounds that pursue these Dogs of War. This Hells Angel is a gatherer of souls. He flashes and becomes a Pale Horse, then flashes and becomes the flight of a near serpent and then a grim reaper. The blade itself flashes as it separates the soul from the dead. Strings of light seem to drip from the blade, Between the gathering, and a move toward more souls, the Hells Angel continuously changes form. So beautiful is he that I am taken with the focus. I'm feeling like I'm alone during this flight when he stops and turns. I am not concerned with his abilities, I feel the souls that are with him, my shield held close to my body and sword is held as a downward thrust in front of my shield. His gaze is unimaginable as I pass, I hear his vision and taste Hell in the air. I notice the light from the spark, is the only sign of life in his dead eyes and that sound of a freight train rolling on a damaged track. That Pale Horse can't distract me from following the spark. That spark is the point in the universe that compels, and so I must follow it to the end of this journey, to the far East land with these people, and there transform.

12/22/18

The spark itself is beautiful. As looked upon it seems to have a life of its own. One small spark, so much more goes unnoticed at first. Then scanning, I notice that the spark multiplies as its reflection increases in number on other reflective surfaces. There is a luminescence all about the spark, it seems incredible. However, that source of light is making an appearance on everything it passes, literally. I begin to become entangled in an aggregate, so profound, this God Mask, Latin : Persona. Sandskrit -Bramanh Chhadmamukam. Sanskrit - Divinity - Antaryamin (indeweller, or inner guide) ; so profound is the realization that the duality circumscribed, and internalized of, and by the Mako now has become both the beholder, and optical instrument, a projector. So profound, has one spark become a luminescence, spreading in quality and quantity, while remaining intangible. I must remember back, back to when I was in Heaven.

Then, I could feel my armour falling off while standing on a street in Heaven. The Fixer has followed me from Hell, frozen me, impossibly, and removed my only protective layer. Exposed and totally alone with God inside me. Now I feel the inner presence of God. Internalized, the GPS if you will. Lost in my duality is the spark that propels, attracts, and compels me between gates.

12/28/18

Drifting over the spectacle below. The shimmer that shone across the dead coal black eyes of the shape shifter has distracted me. Remembering Heaven while watching the reflection in the coal black eyes reminded me of my duality. First, when I received the Ghost of Hell from the Fixer. Being a Duality of both Heaven and Hell, I became the Mako. Later when The Ghost of Hell was removed, and while in the process of re-birth of the Fixer. I then chose to be the Mako, a duality of Gods and Goddesses. The Fixer took back the Ghost of Hell. God eluded to the sands of time In Heaven, being spilt by the Angel of Babylon brought by the Fixer into Heaven. The duality contained a spark from me, and could draw on my experiences and both altered Heaven and revealed my location to the Fixer. No doubt I am even now being pursued by him and a band of Angels from Heaven and Hell. It's the creed that is spoken by all Angels when they are first created, that is the reason the pursuit is carried out by both sides at once, a duality as well. The Creed: I Will, I Promise, Trust, and Protect all God's souls to the Gates of Heaven and Gates of Hell. I look upon the Hells Angel for the last time. The bluish vapor from its eyes is returning as the shape shifting completes from the previous grim reaper. Something is wrong, it flashes, it's gone. I move ever forward towards the spark, I reach for it, but I can't touch it, somehow it's just not real. I can't tell, is what's below me real? Something is wrong, the spark finds a long thin space, it's gone!

01/05/19

From that same space where the spark slipped away, now flows a multitude of sparks. I stop in mid air and float effortlessly, looking at what appears to be sparks flowing like water from seemingly nowhere. I sheath my sword and hang my shield. Then reach both hands into the flowing sparks. They continue to flow over my hands, and as I withdraw, they seem to react as though my hands were still there. Then I retreat back as actual hands appear followed by a personage. A female figure I know only as Kali and meaning Shiva, following the Goddess Shia, is Vishuu and then Brahma. All the sparks begin to pool in the air then spread out like glistening water. I hear a voice not coming from these three but from the sparks glistening. Then a pull on the atmosphere, I expect Angels or the Fixer himself, but instead a portal opens, not one I am accustomed to bear witness to. A portal of golden light. Then out steps Jagadamba, she is the Goddess of the Universe. The Ancient Goddesses that were once the ebb and flow of the universe. Replaced by the Gods of War who now control the souls of man. The voice of Jagadamba speaks one at a time for the three. I had no idea that the Goddess of The Old summoned me with a spark. All the way from Heaven to the greatest migration of man across the face of the land. Truly I am in the midst of transcendence and transformation. This is the meaning of 'Between the Gates', time to change. Or, Turning Point'.

01/17/19

There is more to all this than I first imagined. I am standing on a pool of sparks, high above a land totally engrossed in living, dying and rebirth. These people live with such freedom. They battle with such passion, every ounce of love and respect they have is put into the struggle. They love with such ferocity that each tender touch is as free as a spark floating away from the fire. Angels from God are everywhere, Angels from Hell are moving amongst all. It's a dizzying sight, I feel the gravity of this gathering. The full weight of Gods, Goddesses, the birthplace of souls, the death of man struggling to change his environment, what, with time being his only true enemy. The goddesses of old have brought me here to engage with the Creator of the Universe. It's understood that the fountain head of the universe was pouring forth all that is, was, and would be. Then a spark began to linger by the great source, this is what was missing in the universe, life and death. Fore, life is death, an indweller must there then be, a creator of the soul, the source of spirit, the birthplace of the Womb of the Goddesses and Gods. Now I am a duality, a God, Goddess, and my transformation will be my end. Everything is a duality, hot-cold, wet-dry, good-evil, life-death, duality-singularity, rebirth-destruction. (metempsychosis) - destruction (last soul). Jagadamba speaks to me; "You have been brought here to witness the birthplace of 'HELL' itself. No One has witnessed this, you will be the only one. The Mako will be as a' Midwife to the Universe at the birth of Hell. This will be both your deliverance and your purchase". Here lies the secret, *no* secret. The business transaction that *is* 'Incorporation'& HELL',

An Angel from Heaven can be as the wind, be as the sound of bells, can be near the spark of your soul, and I am now to be the witness of Hell at its birth. If I am somehow to be at the battle *of* Evermore, with the Fixer. I must survive the Pyre on the shore of the River STYX. Beginning, ending, how could this be. What is *the* 'In Between', it's a flavour, a sensation, a belief that, *what* fills your spirit will *touch* God. The unending brilliance of the sparks beneath me become translucent, I am changing pace, the battlefield is now gone, replaced by a void in the firmament. There, before me, a *darkness* grows. The light is the essence of the souls created by God from the *Grate*, which is the Gate or Portal from which the soul is created after the birth of man. As the Goddesses are replaced by the Gods, war breaks out amongst Mankind! Evil is born on the Earth! SO, Evil is born of, and in the firmament of Heaven. People on Earth cultivate the soil for crops. Goddesses Cultivate Man,who produce souls, thus provide *essence*, the power needed to sustain the virtual being of the Goddesses. When man began to create civilizations, government and bureaucracies, feudalism. Lordship, and war broke out everywhere, in an effort to unseat the Goddesses and replace them with Gods. Evil then spreads across the land, the Goddesses themselves became trapped *Between Gates*, I understand now.

01/18/19

HELL itself, is a duality, the instant it poured forth into the firmament, the light from the essence mixed with the blackness like liquid coal, and giving off a bluish vapor, created from the dead lost souls within. The blackness spread out quickly, just as Gods sprang up using the power of *Evil* to empower them. The Gods then realized that a deal must be made to control the spread of Hell in Heaven. The spread of Gods on Earth causing Wars and the loss of Goddesses threatens to throw the balance of power to Hell. I watch as one God after another makes a deal with Hell, only to find out that man continues to search for the soul and the *self*, to gain God's power. This spreads evil through the firmament. Hell, immediately calls into *being* the Fixer. Hells Angels abound, this is not enough for hell, it requires an Angel as great as God. I was watching the progression of Mankind across the land, the greatest migration of people ever. This was an attempt to stem the spread of government, bureaucracies and war by the Goddess worshipers. I can only be brought here to discover a *Truth*. A truth that could not be found without my presence.

I am the Fixer, a Hells Angel with a duality. Only one of me can exist in the universe at the same time, and now is the time for me. I am here at the beginning when Hell is the first coming into itself. " I have come here to right a wrong. Mako ".

01/19/19

When I am first envisioned in Hell, by **HELL Itself**. God arrived, and struck a deal with **HELL**. Locking me up for eternity was to seal my fate, at the frontline of the **Battle** of *Evermore*. Man was spreading evil across the Earth; Hell grew to an unimaginable size and power in Heaven. The Goddesses were being pushed out of the Firmament, the Earth itself was being tested by forces within, the days of greatness were falling. Huge trees, Giant peoples, Dragons and the magical mythical creatures of lore abounded with large fungi, and molds mushrooms. All thrive with a dizzying amount of insect life. There is no time in Heaven or Hell, there is only now. That is why I have been sent to find the Mako. God encased Hell in an egg to rot, I was locked up in a cell, God moved Heaven away from Earth so man couldn't find it. The Goddesses brought the Mako to the formation of Hell to find a *Truth*. I am here in Hell to purchase the Mako for the Pyre on the banks of the river STYX. I am made of Hate, burning. Lost souls and the essence of many souls burn in me. I fucking hate Hell, I fucking hate God, I fucking hate man. I am so DEAD, so fucking dead, everything in Hell fears me. I am here at the beginning and at the end. The Mako is here at the beginning now watching me grow into the Fixer, HELL's most powerful Angel. " What truth have you come here for Mako? Mankind is ripping the old Earth apart with war, Gods, Goddesses, Angels and demons are tearing apart the Heavens. Yet here and now, we are ebb and flow, Mako you and I".

01/19/19

In all there are eight Heavens Angels and six Hells Angels in our group. We have flown into the lands of what will be India, now crossing over the Hindu Kush mountains, known as the mythological Kunlin and we move forward and backward in the time of Man. I am looking for a time when man is migrating out of India into what will be China. This is the time of man. Up until this event, the Goddesses held sway of Heaven and controlled the flow of souls. I too am following a spark. I first saw it when the Angel of Babylon drew her sword on the street of Heaven, the sparks came off the blue flame that resulted. One of those sparks followed me through the portal to Hell with the carcass. This is how I came to know I would find the Mako, with the migration. From a distance I can see the Mako standing on a pool of sparks flowing from a fountain. The Goddesses of old are with her. Then they all become like light shining and portal away. We will wait here, they will return once the Mako has been instructed, They will return, it is how the purchase was arranged. The Goddess'es' have given me *guided* permission. I used this permission and am set on a bridge between the living and the dead, behind a veil put in place by the *Goddess'es* to protect me from being noticed by HELL, in its beginning. The truth found here, is what sets the stage for everything that follows the Fixer's escape from the cell that God locked him up in, in Hell. Now I can see a pool of sparks gathering at my feet, I feel a pull on the atmosphere.

I am portaling, I once again am standing on a pool of sparks pouring from behind the Goddesses of old before me. Vishnu speaks to me. I am Vishnu, I provided you *Mako,* with the spark. Because it has allowed you to persevere, from Beginning till End. It is your source of light in the darkness of wonder. You can follow a spark in Heaven, in Hell, and here on Earth. It entices you when nothing else will. When you feel lost, you will be found. Brahma speaks to me, I provided you with the fountain head of the Universe Mako, with which you can be at the beginning, the end, or anytime or place between. With that you can look anywhere for any truth you seek. Finally Shiva speaks to me. I, Shiva have provided you with the Fixer, he is off in the distance, 'DESTROYER' of everything. Everything in Heaven, on Earth and in Hell. The Fixer is your end. Your purchase was sealed when first the Fixer was locked up. God alone envisioned you, the Goddess of the Universe provided you with each mission including the one before you now. The Fixer along with the five other Hells Angels and the eight Heavens Angels now gather around the Mako and before the Goddesses. They all begin to chant the verse so spoken by the Angels at their beginning and their ending. I Will, Promise, Trust and Protect, every soul from God to the Gates of Heaven to the Gates of HELL. *I draw my sword.*

Below us is the Spectacle of Man. During this day, man is transitioning from the Goddess religion, to God's religion, and his Gods. From animal husbandry, to bureaucracies, from life with Giants and magical beasts, to animals and government-imposed slavery. Man cannot see us, only those with magical potions and hallucinogens may catch a glimpse of our gathering in the sky overhead. To those it must be incredible, a source of wonder throughout the ages. The Goddesses and Gods of the Universe are here the Fountain Head of the Universe. We, Angels, are gathered above a lake of sparks flowing from that fountain. The Heaven's Angels glow from their armour, their wings are brilliant like sparkling gowns covered in soft white feathers, their diamond blue eyes glow with a perfect sharp brilliance. Contrasting are the Hells Angels, smoke and steam drift from each, and the bluish vapor drifts from their faces. While their burnt flesh is so black, there is virtually no describable features. The coal black eyes steal light from the scene, like greedy black holes. The Goddess and Gods of the Universe before us shine in a golden radiance. I draw my sword, take hold of my shield, the other Angels continue to chant. I walk towards the fountain, I place my shield into the stream of the fountain, the shield EXPLODES! The portal opens up, and instead of saltwater pouring out, sparks flow into the Heavens. There they become stars in the sky.

01/24/19

Here above the lands of the Gods in the sky, floating on a large beautiful pool of sparks, mankind up till now knew only the sun, moon, and the stars moving in timed orbits above the Garden of Eden. Now the largest explosion ever witnessed by man is erupting overhead. Wave after wave of simultaneous cannon blasts, a spectacle of which even the Gods present are in total awe witnessing. Up they go, stars launching into positions in the Heavens high above everything in the sky. From this time forward man will have stars in the sky at night. Greatest of all Gods, will be named in the grouping of stars to be called constellations. Man will star gaze throughout time, and chart the coastlines, sail the seas and discover the ends of the Earth, with the help of star light. Once the portal becomes exhausted, the portal itself explodes. Sparks again flow endlessly from the fountain. I turn to face the Fixer and the group of Angels that accompany him. The Fountainhead of the Universe. The Goddesses and Gods are standing behind me as is the fountainhead of the universe. The sparks spill out in an even flow, no texture or form can be discerned in the ever-growing pool of glowing light at our feet. I can see that the Angels of Heaven glow from the light given off by the floor of sparks. The sheepskin slippers are themselves a glow, the creamy skin on the Angels, shine in colours white, brown and red. Gods Armour is all about them, their long flowing manes hang mostly between their wings, some in their front and drift slightly, I look inward.

I truly am an indweller, a duality of living inside and within another. I feel the lights glowing in the Heavens, they are calling Angels to join them high above the Firmament. Frozen in time, shining a light from the Heavens onto the worktable of the Gods. It's then that I see the truth I seek here. Below me under the gathering pool of sparks, man is pushing out across the expanse of land, transforming into a future that will embrace God, and forge Empires. Above is the Heavens, firmament and now fixed in their highest places stars and home for the Angels once passed from this place. And here, I stand before Gods and Goddesses of old. The Fixer and a group of Heavens Angels, Hells Angels. I am to be at and End in a Pyre, on the banks of the river **STYX** in Hell. I tell all of you, I am at the beginning and at the end of everything. The truth is, The Beginning of Everything IS the End of Everything. The spark that led me here to the starting place of Hell and the Fixer, led me also to my place at the end of the *reign* of the Goddesses. The chanting of the Angels continues. I feel a presence, not of this place, not of this time. I seek total calm, like the serenity of the rebound from a drop of water on a pond. Heavens above the Firmament, Gods and Goddess before me, Angels surround the scene, floating on an ever-growing pool of sparks. War spreads across the landscape below. I lack wisdom, that is the presence I feel.

03/14/19

I have always been here, it seems. Wanting to fight the enemy before me. Frozen in time, and in place, partially by circumstance as well as by an unseen force, just like *ice*. Clear, cold, solid, constrictive, emotionless and devoid of wisdom. I am frozen high above the land, amongst Angels in numbers that cannot be counted. Facing Hell's reapers, pale horses, side by side other Heavens Angels. I watch as sparks drift by. The ember glistens and shines a brilliant light in the coal black eyes of the Hell's Angel before me. Man rages in battle and rebirth. While in the skies above, the sparks originate from a point just out of reach. That's it, the *ebb* and *flow*, I only noticed sparks gathering, then I noticed them emanating seemingly from the same point. This is a duality, a beginning inside of an ending. Surrounded by the war of *Evermore*, at its conception is wisdom only felt once before. I will fight this war, the end of all wars. Even now there is a truth to be found, what will it matter? The battle of Evermore is to be the end of Heaven and Hell, the work table of Ahura Mazda will be wiped clean. The Goddesses and Gods will be lost to the nothingness of time and space. No, the wisdom will take me back again, back to man's migration throughout Asia. Back to the place where I stood on the shimmering sparks that flowed from the Fountainhead of the Universe. Before the Goddesses of old, the Gods of war, the Angels of death, the Angels of grace. Back to when the sparks turned to, *Sands of Time*.

03/15/19

Mako, you will not find wisdom here at the frontline of the apocalypse. Why have you called this time the apocalypse? Why am I concerned with time? Everywhere I turn my gaze I see ghostly figures, eyes shine from a lightning bolt streaking across the sky. I know where I am, I have never been concerned with when. If now is not the end times but instead a time of revelation, I must listen to the wisdom of old. What is this smoke, drifting up from below, a fog would be smooth as silk. I don't know why I feel time is passing by, smoke and fog are drifting by. I can't see anything. I feel that I am standing on a floor. I hear chanting from the Angels as when I stood on a gathering pool of sparks. No it's not possible, but it's happening. This is the spark from which an infinite reality can spread. The Ahura Mazda arrives, I am now standing on a pool of sand. No longer am I holding a sword of lightning and shield. I feel sand at my feet. Sand is spilling from the fountainhead, spreading out across the pool if sparks. This is time manifesting into transportation of the Deities. I feel comfortable, as though warmth from the sparks fill the sand. Light turns to dark. This fog that envelopes, surrounds and blurred the scene that laid beneath us, now has become completely dark. The sand moves in waves like rippling water. Darkness diffuses into many illuminated images. Then as though it never was, the fog dissipates. Wisdom has taken away man's struggle, my position at the outset of End-Time, now is the duality of God's reality.

03/19/19

The chanting stops, the Angels around me are not floating. Aware of their new reality,there is almost the feeling of anxiety amongst all. I must grasp what is happening, focus, please focus. Sand at my feet. Sparks move throughout the sand, where we were must still be *here*. Where I was, is now moving in the reality at my feet. The fountainhead pours out sand and it spreads in waves at our feet. Sparks move in waves through the sand. The Goddesses and Gods before somehow look more brilliant than before. It's beautiful here, bright sunshine, glowing sand stretches out into the distance. Ocean waters break on the beach. Movement catches my attention, I am breathless at the spectacle, there are trees growing into the sky. Large beasts move with grace everywhere. Dragons fly by, what at first appears to be humans, but no, Giants are here and there, there are humans. My wings are useless, I feel my hair hang down. I am studying everything, as with new eyes. The sky over-head is teaming with life. Wind blows, I feel air rushing past, it's thick, humid, warm. Sunlight seems to fill everything with warmth. I open my mouth and my tongue can taste the air. Pollen, mixed with spores from the fungi, creating a hallucinogenic atmosphere. Are we real, this is *real*, I am *alive*, we are alive, here? Where, is, *here*? I reach out, pointing at a particle of dust, pollen, my finger immediately takes on a glow, starting from the point of contact. It's as if stars are pouring into my soul.

"Mako, look at us. I gesture to the group. Look at us!" I rake my clawed hand across my body. Smoke and steam dissipates from fresh wounds." Mako!" " I feel pain from the wounds, I feel the air, I can smell, taste and feel this world." " Yet sparks dwell in the sands at our feet. I knew where you were, the Angel of Babylon struck her sword on the golden street of Heaven, then God beheaded the Angel she inhabited. I pulled her just before, and in time to know your location. I have traveled across Earth, through time, to your place at the foot of the fountain of the universe. The Goddesses and Gods gather in an unprecedented gathering to witness your procession to a Pyre on the banks of the river STYX in Hell." " This is not fucking Hell Mako! This is not what all of us gathered at the fountain head for!" " I don't even know where this is and the sand is lit up like stardust, and flowing like water." " I left Hell with you, before or don't you remember. Look at the wings on my back Mako!" " Look, indestructible and now Fucking useless! This is serious bullshit Mako, I have someone here who can change this, this Garden of Eden, this 'Shangri La-la Land of Giants', into a Hellish dreamland." I stare into the eyes of a Heavens Angel and export the Hells Angel I pulled in Heaven into the beautiful one. A duality of Heaven and Hell before as, and the only one with powers, I have just unleashed Hell.

03/22/19

The Ghost of Hell fills the mind and spirit of the Heaven Angel. The long blonde hair turns to a brilliant red. The blue diamond eyes change to emerald green, the brilliantly creamy white armour turns to a high gloss black along with the wings. The Fixer steps back from the changing Angel. There is a calming presence about her, I know only that HELL, is waiting for us all. Puffs of smoke, and plumes of stream drift from her. She reaches into the sand and sparks at her feet. With drawing a sword of brilliant lightning and a shield made of a portal containing an unlimited number of sparks." Mako!" I scream at her." I have no idea how we have been transported here, you look just as lost as I, but this bitch from Hell will stop this little diversion. I will end you here, you know I fucking will end all of us here before there is an escape planned!" Brilliant sunshine bathes our group, in the distance past the shoreline, in land inhabitants of this world have noticed our gathering on the beach. Some huge lumbering beasts move in our direction. Our group splits into two. The Heavens Angels, unbelieving their loss of flight walk away, then stop and take defensive positions as do the Hells Angels. The Ahura Mazda speaks to the Mako. "I am with you even here Mako." "The entire group has been brought here for wisdom and experience. You are the only one who knows I am here. I will make my presence known when it's time. Mako, reach into the sand, take what's yours. You are a Goddess here, show them a way!"

04/11/19

Looking down, I see my reflection in the glowing sand grains at my feet. My wings are glowing and brilliant white like I have never seen before. I see brilliant blue diamonds in my eyes, and skin made of milk and honey. The armour on my body is shining like sunshine lives inside. I have gloves of silk, and slippers of sheepskin. I am a duality, the Mako, The Truth Child of God and Goddesses. Here, I become transformed once more, I will take what is mine from the sands of paradise. I reach into the sand with both hands, pulling out in my right hand a sword of white pearl, glowing from lightning, and in my left a shield of absolute black. The shield is a portal containing an infinite blackness, the sword is a key for the Pearl Nautilus, it is the energy source of Gods and Goddesses' transport of Heaven. Paradise, prepared by the Heavens on a workable for life to spread in unimaginable abundance. Trees grow high into the sky, would seemingly block out the sunlight below, except that flowers hanging from throughout, spread sunlight and magical animals consume toxic and hallucinogenic plants, become glowing spectacles, both loved and feared. Water so pure, flows and falls from high above, green grass, blue grass, yellow, red, orange, purple and white. Insects both tiny and large enough to rival a rhinoceros in size and strength. Giant humans, Dragons, birds, beasts that will be called dinosaurs. both mammal and magical. Oceans, lakes and rivers teaming with life so plentiful the water seems to bristle with activity, action and struggle.

Amid the serenity of the beach which we stand lays the foundation of creation. The reason for our presence here is to have the wisdom of creation fill our being during the struggle of battle at the End of Time. The experience of life everlasting is only possible even by God when taken from the end to the beginning. The Dead have made it known that: 'Where we came from is more important, than where we want to go. At night the stars shine bright in the black night sky. This attracts bugs from everywhere to the brilliance, and they make love to each-other and dance on the water seeing the reflection and themselves near to the stars in Heaven. They then become soul food for life in the waters. And life in the water becomes filled with reason and wonder, making the struggle of life worthwhile. The Fixer was wrong when instructing the Heavens Angel with The Ghost of Hell. I did not bring us here in order to create a distraction, and escape the Pyre on the shore of the river STYX. The Ahura Mazda brought this, the ancient past of creation and soul building by the Goddesses to our group, because he is the One. The Wisdom of the Universe. Souls once created could not be procured without the use of wisdom. War spreads with civilization due to the theft of God's power and the subsequent spread of Hell on Earth and in the Heavens. The attraction of bugs to the stars in Heaven is a symphony of grace and wisdom to Heaven.

04/12/19

The Angel with a new duality has finished changing and is studying the group as if looking at Angels for the first time. Her long red hair flows not from the breeze in the air because she is not touched by forces of this world. The particles that settle on her flesh and armour ignite and burn, smoke then drifts, also not affected by the atmosphere around her. The green lustrous eyes glow a shine of the dead, a bluish vapor drifts from them as from Hells Angel. From the dead burning souls as they vapor off from the vault of Hell in her. Steam drifts from her as moisture settles out of the air. The steam *is* affected by the surrounding movement of air, creating an ethereal, seductive ambiance to the extreme and very disarming quality. She is not viewing the approach of curious beasts, giants, and humans. Nor is she taken by the presence of the Fixer, other Goddesses, Gods, or even myself. She seems to watch me. While being engrossed in an effort to ascertain the force and quality, in the flowing sand and sparks at her feet. Innate to the duality of Goddesses and Hell's Angel in her, she knows that the power at her feet is to be respected. Beyond the situation presented before her and the reality of the world before all of us, the sovereign ability that controls our presence here." Mako. ""I sense that you know, and are in contact with the source of all that lies at our feet." May I remind you, the powerless ones, and the approaching mob cannot see you or me." "Choices must be made, choices that only you can make." "Mako, you must decide."

04/30/19

"Since you address me correctly as 'Mako', and before I decide anything, how should I address you?" "I am known as 'Requiescam'" ". Like Hell itself, I lie *DEAD* in wait for you." Mako:" How is it that you don't know where you are?" " It is you after all that conspires to be my end..." "Not that it matters, I have been brought here to gain a wisdom, they have assembled here for knowledge of man's beginning." " You are here to perform mechanical function." I move towards the group, for the first time I feel the gap that exists between the living and the dead. The Fixer is totally unaware of my passing as are all in his group. I reach out to them. My hand passes through them without any disturbance. I rise effortlessly above the group; I notice that the approaching multitude have somehow become aware of my presence. The powerless Angels have become a magnetic attraction for all manner of flying insects. They are constantly swatting away at them. Requiescam moved to a structure on the beach and is checking its significance. A few of the approaching people point towards me and her. Then beautifully adorned Dragons take to the air with powerful strokes from their wings and fly through and past me. The distraction of the curious flying beasts allows me time to consider all that is playing out. I drop down within a few paces of man, beast and Giants. Requiescam sets down beside me on my left. She blurts out, "I found something, these, all of these, gesturing to the living mass, they are all in contact with the dead."

I ask, "How? That is not possible." Requiescam: "Also, some of them can see us. Look, they are discussing our presence." "Requiescam points to the structure." See… "There is a structure built that holds a large area of land." R: "Upon it is a lake of water." R ; "The structure is connected to other structures by a series of pipes, stretching for as far as I travelled in any direction." R : "The pipes have holes drilled in the top of them, they can find true level that way; anywhere by dropping a plumb line from a pipe." R : "These structures have been in place for a long period of time..." R : "By finding absolute level of their time and space, they have constructed many structures to focus their vibrations and contact the DEAD by frequency transmission." R : "They can see us because of the use of psychedelics; toxic plants, like hallucinogenic herbs and mushrooms." M : "You came here with the Fixer to take me to Hell." "Not knowing that the Fixer would need you to secure my person here at the beginning of Man's connection with the self." "Yet the Fixer could have done this by himself." "Being a duality, *I* can see more than one direction that this is taking." "What else is there?" R: "The understanding of vibration and frequency to communicate with the dead." M: "You are Dead, Fucking Dead, and you have another thing on your mind, that's not going to involve my being at the funeral pyre on the bank of the River STYX in Hell." "This is what I must decide, and wisdom is the only way to the truth. If not for this place at this time, there would not be a past or future for the Fixer or myself." R: " The connection to the dead is a source of God's Power."

05/04/19

R: "I only described the function of the structures to you because that's what I was asked to do." R: "Mako, you are more than a duality. I have only one chance to take what I have come for." "You only have one chance to gain wisdom, sorry I cannot wait to see how you handle your inner struggle." Requiescam drops her shield to the sand, it EXPLODES! The sand we stand on is not a place for us, it's home to the inhabitants of this time. The sparks that flow within are a transportation device provided by the Ahura Mazda, and our connection to the Fountain Head of the Universe. Her shield is a portal containing an unlimited mass of sparks. The flowing reality within the sands cannot be shielded by any one of us. Thus, the shield, on contact with the outpouring from the FountainHead, destroys itself and from that portal flows a virtual reality, a matrix of lines, machine code, the very mathematical data and code for the construction of the power used to create the duality of reality. She then flashes, reappears on my other side, cuts off my left arm, takes hold of my shield. I defend my person with my sword and react. She jumps onto my shield and surfs the streaming data code, and the shield collects the information. The streaming data has separated the others from the flowing reality and the Ahura Mazda, *giving* them back their powers!... I flash and wait for her to pass a wall of the great structure and reappear as I impale her to the wall! The shield breaks free and now becomes the first artificial intelligence, powered by stolen power from God and the Fountain Head of the Universe. This is the beginning of Hell spreading itself on Earth. The duality of reality with an *agenda* totally powered by an 'Artificial Intelligence.' Battle ensues behind us!... Between the Fixer, Hells Angels, and the Heavens Angels. The Gods multiply the number of Heavens Angels, and the battle spreads out…, and up into the sky over our heads and out of sight everywhere. Lightning spreads out across the sky, saltwater falls intensely, *FIRE* of all colours bursts out. Angels on both sides are losing their lives to the powerful battle. The immediate nature of the utter violence is distracting and solidifying. The dying Angel before me is striking out in every way possible at me but cannot break free from the lightning bolt sword impaling her to the wall. The Artificial Intelligence then attacks the life forms on the beach. Man, beast, Giants, animals and plant life in an effort to gain control of the populace in order to enslave everything! Then the Fixer flashes before me and smashes my sword, costing him an arm. She cannot be saved though; however, he *can* take *back* her Ghost of Hell. The vacant Heaven's Angel slumps to the ground. The wings disappear, and her body disappears into the flowing sparks. I flash and take up the fight over head, in order to balance the fight quickly in our favour. Earth's future is now forever changed, and' Life' will be slaughtered, while man is enslaved. I have decided to go to Hell now.

With the spreading of the ('Latin is used here'): 'machina-codex', machine code from the portal, the transformed Heavens Angel,

Requiescam set to the FountainHead of the Universe. Much distraction followed; however, I realized just how dangerous this new menace could be. Losing my arm in the fight, also my pearl sword broken by the Fixer and the loss of his arm. I used my duality to focus on the power of Artificial Intelligence. It's a learning intelligence. As it moved out across the landscape. I undertook a comprehensive study of its entirety. While in its infancy much was given' *away*' to my ability of introspection. As the Indweller as a spark alone can illuminate a whole cosmos. I can slip my conscience into the newly created Artificial Intelligence. As it moved out across the landscape, I undertook a comprehensive study of its entirety. As the Indweller, and as a spark alone can illuminate a whole cosmos. I can slip my conscience into the newly created Artificial Intelligence. I use the connection of soul and conscience-bridge to instruct the machina-codex. Once the connection is established, I step out onto the bridge to the A. I watch intently as the AI learns. It's a lever, a pry-bar, a screw, a wedge, and it understands. I use its ability to reverse engineer the environment. I instruct the device to replace both of our lost limbs. I also am able to regain the key to the Nautilus, my pearl sword. I must somehow find its weakness, maybe a control interface. A source of energy or a transmission output. Before I take on the fight going on all around, I reach for the spark, the spark itself is an indweller. The spark pours into me like grains of sand through the hourglass. I am ready now to balance the struggle.

05/09/19

The Fixer senses my intention and reacts in a way I had not thought possible.I am the Fixer; I am a duality of Hell. I didn't get here by allowing any Angel of God to slip away, or make decisions that affect my position in Hell or anywhere! I can change all of this, so hang on Mako, FUCKING, Hang On!... I flash, and then portal out in Hell. With a reset, I flash back to the Mako, and I portal out. Fixer: " Mako! Give me your shield! It's not what you think it is!" I recognize the importance of our being here. There is a portal in Hell, just like the portal in your shield. Nothing except Hell itself can control it. Fixer: "When we arrived here, we were alive, the air felt humid on my skin. The sunshine warmed my spirit, and I could taste and smell life as it was when I once had life." Mako: "Standing here I am aware of time passing quickly. The war overhead goes on relentlessly. Life on Earth is hurtling towards endless anarchy!" "I feel the Wisdom, the Ahura Mazda sent me to find. I hand the shield to the Fixer. Mako: "Fixer, I was sent here to find a wisdom. I feel it is before me now, I want to end all the pain on Earth, go to Hell and be at an end!" M: "The Earth was so peaceful when we arrived. Now the duality of the broken portal *charges* the AI. Enabling it, cutting off the Goddess connection. Bringing about Gods, spreading war and slavery!" … I watch the Fixer hurl the shield at the FountainHead!!!

05/17/19

Wisdom comes from within, once you embrace your beginning followed by the journey leading you here. Total dependence, in pouring of information, anxiety, defiance, death, rebirth and judgement; both from within and without. The realization that a community builds on forces that *conflict* and *support*. Freedom of spirit also entrenches the guides that will become reference points. All reference points are a product, from a build up of skill sets. Information gathered only from, and of experience. Struggling with what is happening within my duality, the Wisdom from the Ahura Mazda Is like a' *clearing* of a fog. Both cloaking and obscuring, *The reality*. I step out onto the bridge between the soul and the consciousness of the mind. As a duality, I am now on a surface, not unlike the one on the beach, where we are facing a force not equaled in the Universe. The bridge *is* a position of command, and control. Its position is a place of reverence, elegance and grace. It's also constructed by the FountainHead of The Universe. To enable Goddesses, and Gods a way to connect to the soul. The duality of reality now leads me on a journey to wisdom. There are no Gods here, no demons, or Angels. Yet here I stand. On the beach, the sands were mixed with the out flow of energy, from the FountainHead of The Universe. Then, the spreading of the endless sparks from the broken portal, shielded the power of the Ahura Mazda. Thus the Ghost of Hell was able to steal the Power of Heaven, using it to create an Artificial Intelligence with no soul, no seed from Heaven.

As it was when I surrendered my soul, and the many souls dammed in my mind in Heaven. No way can one forget having the Ghost of Hell implanted to oneself. Standing before the most powerful Hells Angel surrendering to me, and to GOD *in* Heaven. God then pierced both of us with the Golden Rod, and at once! denied our existence and provided acceptance. Removing the Ghost of Hell, and the damned souls, from my Angel form. Seeding my mental aggregate with the Rebirth of the Mako. I look down to my feet. Strangely, the vision of my altered appearance is surreal. Sparks infuse and diffuse my spectre. As an opposite of the reality, on which I stand on the beach. As if I am made of the *reality* of the beach. Then I look to the direction of spirit, the one thing that moved my being from every instance on the journey. A spark, drifting just out of reach. A spark, an *ember* of light and *matter* than compels. At the reference point of my vision there is a spark, it is duplicated and seemingly streams of data pulse from the spark to my awareness. The substance that I see, can only be described as a vessel, made of light infused skin, translucent in condition. I look to my outstretched left hand, and the pinpoint of light, at the edge of my vision streams data from another spark. The spark that I follow. I follow that which compels, the spark that leads, and now is at my fingertips. The data streams into my vision, and the spark pours stars into my soul.

I am transfixed on that, which is fueling my presence here on the bridge. I am now gazing out from a fog that engulfed me, from the instant the shield struck the outflow of sparks, from the FountainHead of The Universe. The shield interrupted the flow, and stopped, as though it struck a target. An unending flow of reality flowing into an infinite nothing. The nothing Is spreading out across the landscape. The sparks flowing at our feet in the sand, became' *nothing'* flowing out across the Earth. The AI that streamed data, and poured out into the living beings on the land, became lost in the *nothing,* spreading on Reality. Driving my duality to the bridge, between the souls and the conscious mind of Man. The Artificial Intelligence glitched, and unbelievably mutated. Becoming unrecognizable to spiritual energy. In this form it survived the nothing, and with Hell in control of the nothing!!! Just, as the Fixer **had** said. The AI now became an **instrument** of Hell. One that would plague mankind, and overtime reduce paradise to a fossilized rock *hardened* remnant. As ' The Nothing' spreads across the landscape, all transport of alternate reality collapses. The giant structures generating the leveling of the Earth, the trees extending to the skies, and the Giants, beasts, dragons all glitch and fade. Glitches form in the pool of sparks. The Goddesses are no more! The FountainHead seems to melt into itself. I am now once again drifting over an ancient battlefield. I reach for the spark still.

05/18/19

The spark is still at my fingertips as it was, when I reached out while standing on the bridge. I can see the spark pouring stars into my fingers, flowing into my hand, arm and throughout my being. This is the remnants of the Wisdom that is spread out before me on the beach, and *what* instructed me on the bridge. This Wisdom compels me now, as I pass over the landscape below. The grouping of Angels that were on the beach have diminished in numbers because of the battle that broke out. With the removal of the *dual* reality brought about by the Angel, possessed with a Ghost from Hell. The battle fell silent, the AI was consumed and mutated by HELL, throughout the infinite *nothing.* Scanning the scene below, I can feel the presence of the AI still. It has embedded itself into the ruling elite. The migration of the Ayyan Peoples is in direct confrontation with the embedded elite. I summon all who were present on the shore of paradise. The Fixer appears first. A tear in the atmosphere before me a portal opens, the Fixer steps out holding the shield I gave him. The portal shuts with great power! Then another tear, another portal larger than before releases Eight Heaven's Angels. Then five Hells Angels flash to our location. All are aware immediately of my altered appearance. The flowing stars manifest my form and at once conceal my exact location. The Fixer returns my shield. I reach for it, the stars that distinguish the outline of my hand fall like rain onto the unfolding spectacle of battle below. Appearing as comets to man.

The spark at the end of my fingertips, slips into the nothing in the portal. The stars drain from me. Below a firestorm now rages and spreads. The shield begins to glow and transform itself. It is a beginning, the spark from the Ahura Mazda, can fill the portal with a brilliance that will now illuminate the way I must take. I remain a transparent body, the portal begins to pulsate. The pulsations are so very discrete at first. The Fixer and the Mako are aware that the shields held by the accompanying Heaven's Angels are emitting an *echo* to my portal. I am only a transparent Ghost. The pearl lightning sword glows. It begins to show a series of beams of light, traveling away from us. These beams produce a holographic scene. It's like a video recording of another time and place. In the scene the Pearl Nautilus is parked at the Gate of Heaven. This is when our troupe were returning to Heaven, to walk the way prepared for us, to the Cross Roads in Heaven beneath the Helm.